LITTLE SIMON

An imprint of Simon & Schuster Children's Publishing Division
1230 Avenue of the Americas, New York, New York 10020
Copyright © 1978 by Eric Carle. Eric Carle's name and signature logo type are trademarks of Eric Carle. All rights reserved including the right of reproduction in whole or in part in any form. LITTLE SIMON and colophon are registered trademarks of Simon & Schuster. Manufactured in Malaysia. First Little Simon edition 2002.
2 4 6 8 10 9 7 5 3 1
ISBN 0-689-84964-8

t! A Giant!

ey   Singapore

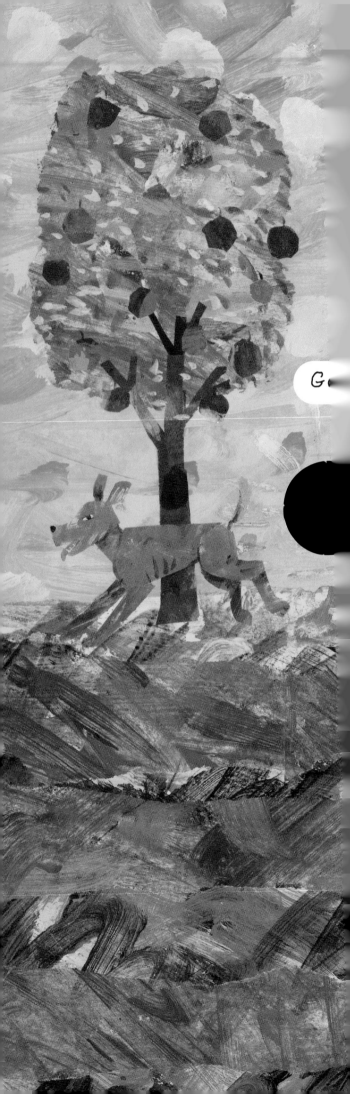

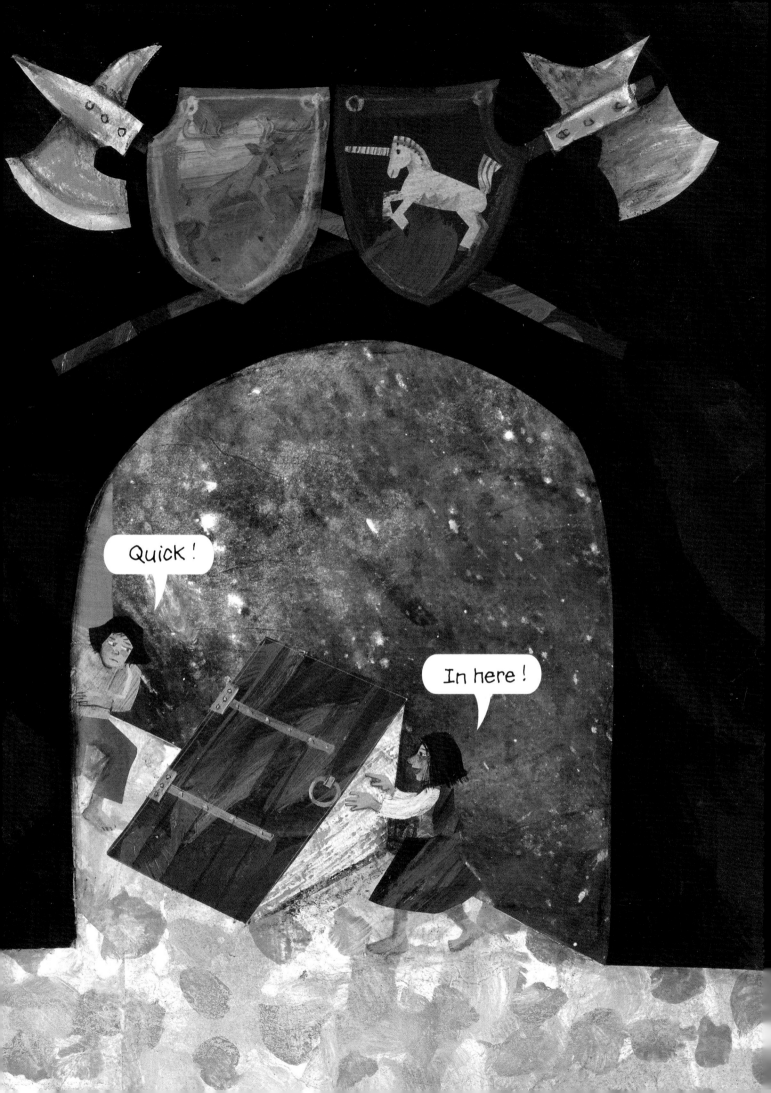

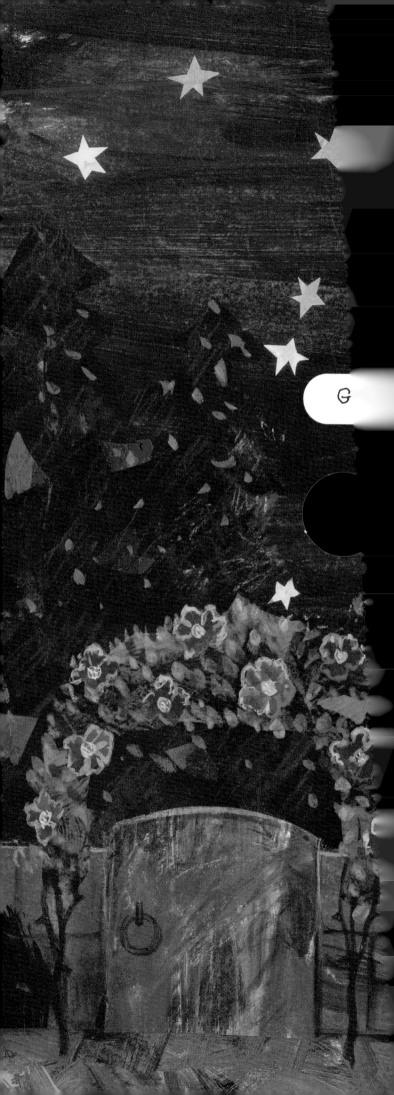

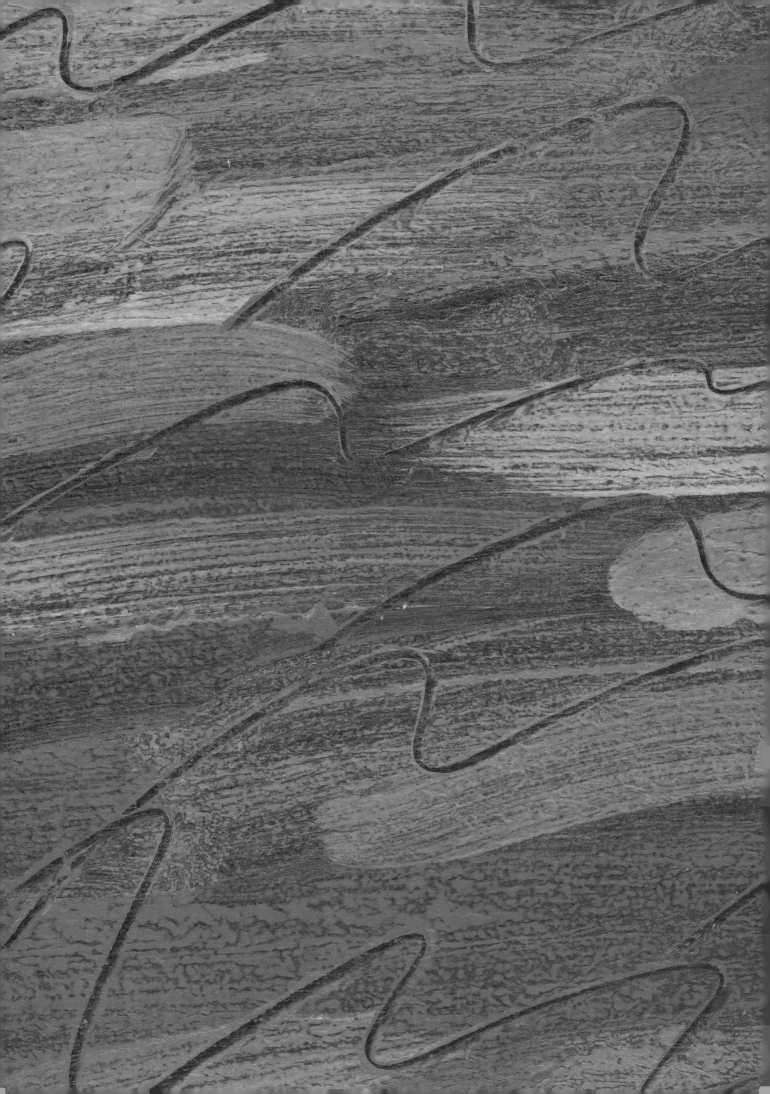